J 598.15 V225h
Vande Griek, Susan, 1950- author.
Hawks kettle, puffins wheel : and other
 poems of birds in flight

Hawks Kettle, Puffins Wheel

And Other Poems of Birds in Flight

Susan
Vande Griek
&
mark
Hoffmann

Kids Can Press

Hawks Kettle, Puffins Wheel

Birds fly — well, most do.
But did you know that they also
kettle, mob, wheel and dive,
as well as many other things besides?

Always, and in their own special ways,
birds are on the move.

Birds' bodies are built for flying. Their streamlined shape helps them move easily through the air. Their wings are made of strong feathers and hollow bones that are relatively light. And birds have special chest muscles that power their flapping wings. By jumping or running, and then flapping their wings, birds produce thrust to take off and start flying. Air rushes over the top of their curved wings and creates lift — the force that keeps them aloft. Their tail feathers control steering, speed and balance as the birds maneuver through the air.

Puffins Wheel

In the cool air
over the northern sea,
the adult puffins
in black and white
are wheeling,
wheeling
round and round.

Circling over sea
and island cliffs,
circling near nests
they've burrowed
in turfed ground,
the puffin wheel
goes round and round.

Birds drop out
to fish and feed.
Others lift up
to flap and fly.

Puffins freewheeling in open sky.

Atlantic puffins
wheel, flying round and
round in large circles, above
the sea and their island nesting
colonies. This may be their way to
confuse and scare off predators, such
as gulls, that could be after a solitary bird
or venturesome chick. As the adult puffins
wheel, some of them will drop down to
fish, carrying back the catch in their
bills to feed their young. Others
will fly up from the colony to
join the wheel.

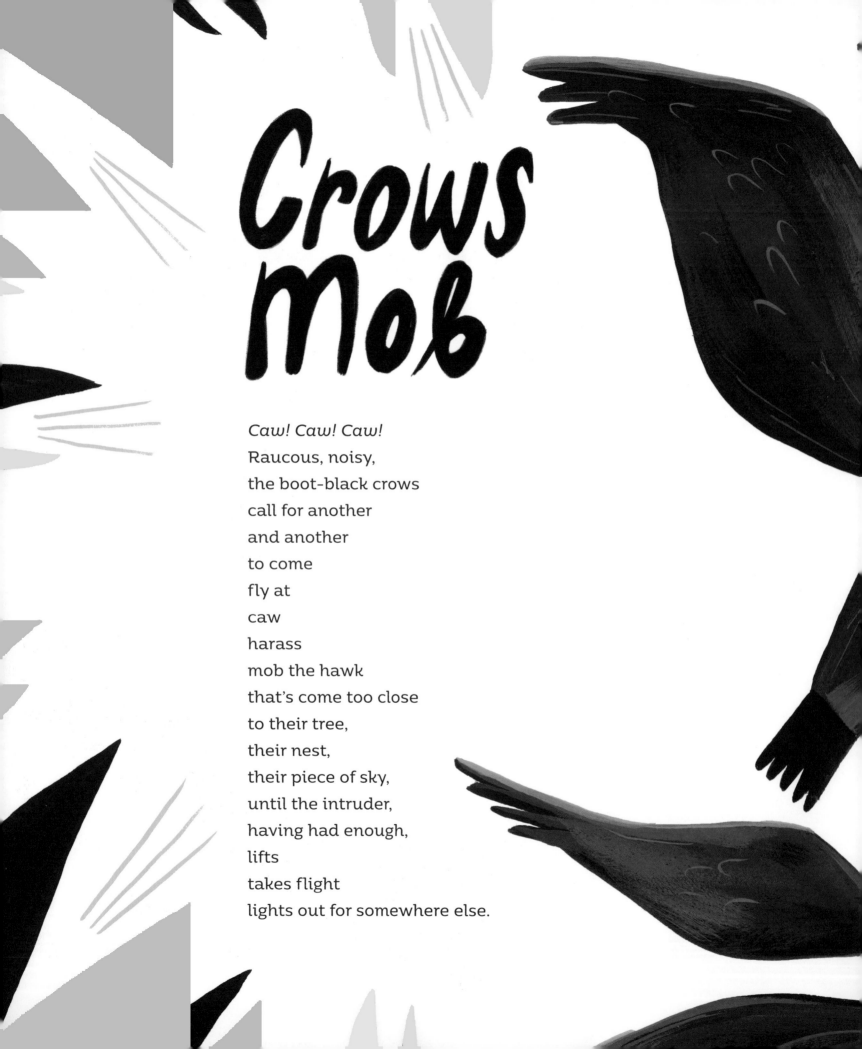

Crows Mob

Caw! Caw! Caw!
Raucous, noisy,
the boot-black crows
call for another
and another
to come
fly at
caw
harass
mob the hawk
that's come too close
to their tree,
their nest,
their piece of sky,
until the intruder,
having had enough,
lifts
takes flight
lights out for somewhere else.

American crows will mob a threatening animal, such as a hawk, owl or cat, that enters their territory. More crows may join in when they hear the alarm calls of other mobbing crows. The birds fly and caw at the intruder, continually harassing it until they chase off the animal. In some cases, they might even physically attack the predator with their feet or beaks. Other birds also use mobbing behavior, including terns, jays and chickadees.

In fall, the geese
    are flying south
        in groups that gather
           and stretch out.
              Skeining cross the autumn sky,
          a moving V, a vocal flight,
      a skein of geese
      a-honking out the
change of season.

Geese Skein

Canada geese often fly in a V formation when migrating south in the fall and back north in spring. The flying flock, usually made up of families, is called a skein. The skein allows the birds to save energy on their journey, since air coming off each bird's wings gives lift to the bird behind. The geese will change leads so that one bird does not get overly tired. The skein formation may also help the geese easily keep track of one another.

Peregrines Stoop

High
and fast
the falcon flies —
wings beating,
body banking —
till its keen,
watchful eye
spies prey below.

It makes its dive.

Down it drops —
so swift,
so steep.
Down it goes
in a dizzying stoop,
then strikes
its prey
with powerful feet.

Success!
It eats.

Peregrine falcons fly high, scanning above and below for prey with their very sharp eyesight. When the falcon spots its prey, usually a smaller bird, it rises up and then drops down in a steep, fast dive called a stoop. Tucking wings and feet in close, it streamlines its body to plunge and make its kill. A stooping peregrine can reach speeds of more than 300 km (185 mi.) per hour, making it one of the fastest animals on Earth.

Hovering
at feeder,
at flower,
wings beating
so fast
that they hum
with little-bird power.

See this minuscule
might of a bird

float in midair,

a feat
amazing
to behold.

Ruby-throated hummingbirds can hover, staying
suspended in midair, because of the special way
they flap their wings. By moving their wings in an
almost figure-eight pattern, they create lift from
their backward *and* forward strokes. The rapid beat
of their wings (up to seventy times per second!)
also helps them hover. This allows the birds to drink
nectar from delicate flowers. Hummingbirds often
fly backward — the only bird known to do so — to
move away from a flower after feeding.

Hummingbirds Hover

Sandpipers Flock

Sandpipers gather
in the lateness of summer,
peeps by the thousands
flocking together.
Enormous flocks
traveling south,
rest-stopping on mudflats,
feeding on mud shrimp
       when the tide is out.

They lift as one
with flying precision,
white bellies, dark backs
rolling this way and that.
A wave rising from shore
and flocking south.

Semipalmated sandpipers, often called peeps, migrate in flocks of thousands of birds. The flock's size protects the birds from predators. On their long journey, they will rest for several days on sandy or muddy seashores, where they feed on tiny shrimp-like creatures and insects. Whenever the birds take off from the shore, they move together as one, never colliding. The birds flash their light bellies as the flock swoops and turns.

The gannets,
those hungry,
hungry
northern seabirds,
fish to eat,
have their own technique.

Loitering high
above the waves,
a school of mackerel
spotted below,
they dive
headfirst,
wings folded back,
to strike water,
plunge under,
attack and catch
lunch, dinner
or a midday snack.

Gannets Plunge-Dive

Northern gannets are seabirds that feed on small fish, such as mackerel, herring and capelin. They often fly high above the ocean in search of a school of fish. Once they spot their prey, gannets will dive headfirst toward the water, folding their wings in close to increase speed. Their necks and shoulders have special adaptations to protect their bodies as they hit the water. After plunging under, they can swim deep down in pursuit of a catch.

In September
the hawks —
those broad-winged
woodland hunters —
are on the move.
Taking wing
from fall's turning forests,
following upland slopes,
continental coasts,
in great numbers, they migrate.

They're riding the air,
kettling,
soaring high and round
in a warm uplift,
then gliding off
and on
in a southward drift.

A kettle of hawks,
like bubbles in a pot,
boiling up
and out the top.

Hawks Kettle

Broad-winged hawks soar on air currents to conserve energy when migrating. With the help of updrafts (upward-moving air currents) and thermals (columns of warm air rising over cool air), hawks can soar without always having to flap their wings. When the birds have soared high, they will then glide on to find the next air current. A group of hawks circling in these currents is called a kettle, perhaps because the birds look like bubbles rising up in a boiling pot.

Here in the Arctic
on a barren shore,
the nesting, noisy —
kee-kee-kar!
kee-kee-kar! —
arctic terns
go quiet,
lift up
in a rapid swoosh.

A sudden dread.

Is danger near?
A fox,
a gull,
looking to make a meal?

Forked tails,
knifelike wings,
are looping above,
dreading round.

And then,
in a moment,
has danger passed?
Startled terns
drop,
settle back to ground.

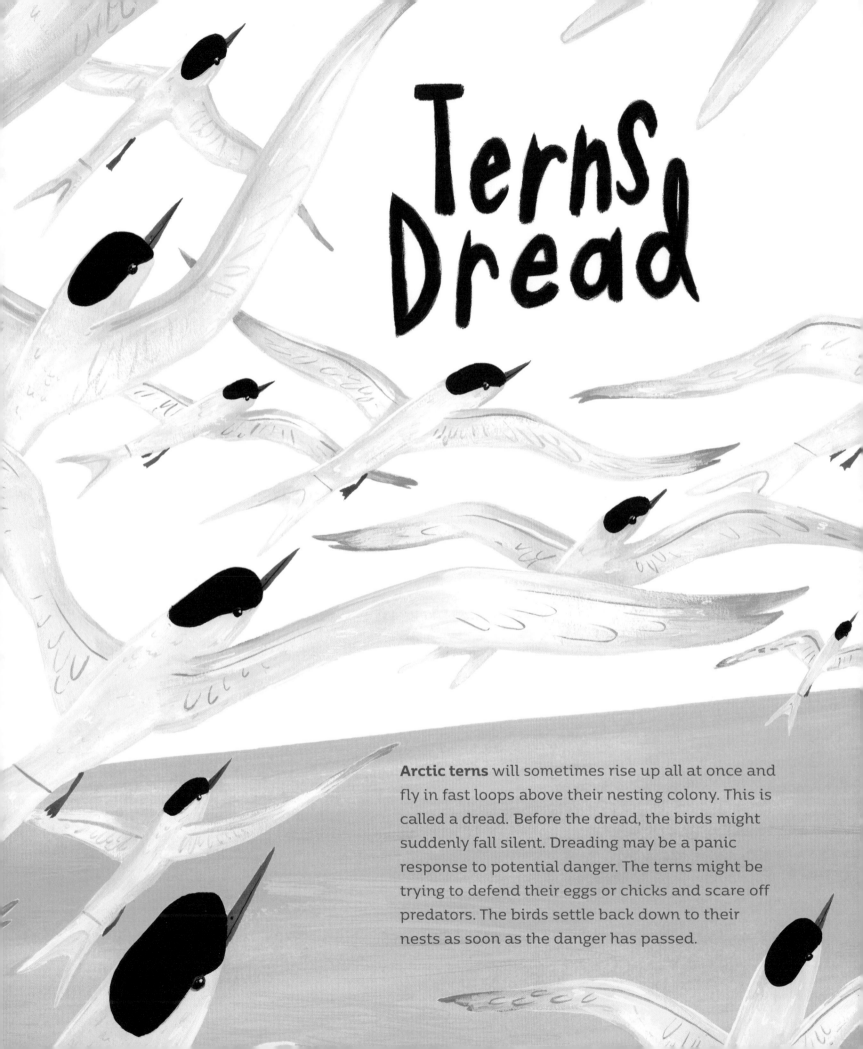

Terns Dread

Arctic terns will sometimes rise up all at once and fly in fast loops above their nesting colony. This is called a dread. Before the dread, the birds might suddenly fall silent. Dreading may be a panic response to potential danger. The terns might be trying to defend their eggs or chicks and scare off predators. The birds settle back down to their nests as soon as the danger has passed.

Starlings

Murmurating starlings —
a starling murmuration —
hundreds, no, thousands
of wing-flapping birds
heard gathering at sunset
to roost, but first
flying close,
swooping together.

A dark, acrobatic
cloud of birds,
twisting, swirling
here, then there —
shape-shifting patterns in the air.

European starlings gather at dusk in the fall, before roosting for the night. They move in unison in a huge flock, called a murmuration. The flock moves quickly back and forth, up and down, creating what looks like a dark cloud shifting in the sky. The mumuration might confuse predatory birds looking to pick off a lone starling. It might also keep the starlings warm when roosting.

murmurate

Sometimes
in courting,
a pair of eagles
flying high
lock together,
talon finding talon,
then tumble
spiral
cartwheel toward earth.

And just when it seems
they might smash
crash
hit the ground,
they break apart,
talon losing talon,
not a second too soon.

SWOOP!

Eagles Cartwheel

Bald eagles often perform an unusual flying feat when they are courting, or looking for a mate. The male and female lock talons while high in the air and then tumble toward the earth. They let go of each other only when they are close to the ground, ending the display. Scientists think these cartwheel moves might be an eagle's way of testing a mate's fitness or of strengthening the bond with a potential mate.

Sitting on a perch,
on a branch with a view,
the wood-pewee waits,
watching the air
for an insect or two.

Quick-quick
it darts out
on fast-moving wings,
catching on the fly
a bite to eat.

Then back to its perch
where it sits up
and waits
for another bug
to pass its way.

Fly out.
Catch.
Fly back.
Repeat.

Flycatching's the way
a wood-pewee eats.

Eastern and western wood-pewees belong to a group of birds known as flycatchers. Flycatching is how some birds capture food. A pewee will sit on a tree branch watching for insects to pass by. The bird will then fly out and snatch the insect from the air before returning to its perch. After eating, it repeats the process. Although these birds do catch flies, the behavior is called flycatching because they catch food while flying.

Pewees Flycatch

Hawks kettle, crows mob,
puffins wheel, gannets dive.

Always, and in their own special ways,
birds are on the move.

More About the Birds in This Book

Atlantic Puffin | *North Atlantic Ocean*

These puffy-looking black-and-white seabirds have bright orange feet and a colorful bill. They nest in burrows, which they dig in grassy areas above northern island cliffs. When not in their nesting colonies, puffins spend all of their time out at sea. Here, they feed on small fish and squid. With fish populations decreasing because of human fishing and climate change, puffin numbers are declining.

American Crow | *North America*

These all-black birds have adapted to live in both the city and country, and to eat many different foods, such as trash, dead animals, berries and seeds. This has helped them survive and multiply. They are one of the most intelligent birds. Social and noisy, crows make an easily recognizable cawing sound, but they have a variety of other calls, too, which they use to communicate with each other.

Canada Goose | *North America*

Canada geese are large brownish birds with long black necks and white chins. They can be found in parks and fields, and by lakeshores. At night, they often rest on water. These wild geese mostly eat seeds, grass and grains. Canada geese make a distinctive honking sound but actually have about thirteen different calls. The babies, called goslings, can even communicate with their parents while still in their eggs!

Peregrine Falcon | *Worldwide*

Fast and skillful, peregrines are excellent hunters. They use their powerful talons and strong beaks to prey on small birds and mammals, and large insects. They nest on ledges, cliffs and even city skyscrapers. These birds have bluish-gray backs, long wings and a dark "mustache" on either side of their beaks. Peregrine falcon populations were under threat but have recovered since the pesticide DDT was banned.

Ruby-Throated Hummingbird | *Eastern North America, Central America*

Ruby-throated hummingbirds can often be found in gardens and meadows. They use their long bills and tongues to drink nectar from flower blossoms or sugar feeders. They have green, glistening feathers and light-colored bellies. The males have distinctive ruby-colored throats. These tiny birds migrate more than 800 km (500 mi.) across the Gulf of Mexico — without stopping! They are the only hummingbird regularly found in eastern North America.

Semipalmated Sandpiper | *North America, Central America, South America*

Sandpipers are small shorebirds with gray-brown backs and light underbodies. Their long black legs and bills, as well as their partly webbed (semipalmated) toes, help them to feed on tidal mudflats and sandy shores. After fattening themselves up for their migration, they fly nonstop from North America to South America. Sandpiper numbers may be declining due to pollution and human disturbance to their flocks while they are resting and feeding.

Northern Gannet | *North Atlantic coasts*

Gannets are large seabirds with big wingspans. These powerful fliers can often glide for long periods of time, skimming just above the waves. They are white with black wing tips and have a light yellow or golden color on the backs of their necks and heads. Gannets nest in large colonies on cliffs and islands, where they are safe from many predators. Except when nesting, they are seldom on land.

Broad-Winged Hawk | *North America, South America*

Broad-winged hawks — with their short, wide wings and short, wide tails — are well suited to fly through the thick forests where they live. When hunting, they perch in trees to watch the ground below. Then, they swoop down to grab their prey, usually small mammals, insects, frogs or toads. They migrate from North to South America in fall, usually in large groups. Their population is numerous but under threat from the destruction of forested areas.

Arctic Tern | *North America, Europe, Antarctica*

These white-and-gray birds sport black caps and forked tails. Terns feed on small fish, shrimp and krill. They can hover over the water until they spot their prey, then dive to scoop it from near the water's surface. Nesting in colonies on Arctic islands and beaches, terns raise their young before migrating south. They are long-distance fliers, migrating from the Arctic all the way to Antarctica, which might be the farthest migration of any bird.

European Starling | *North America, Europe*

Starlings were first brought to New York from Europe in 1890 and have survived and spread in large numbers all over North America — in both cities and the countryside. These very vocal birds are often seen in small flocks. Their blackish feathers, often with white spots, have a sheen to them. They feed on insects, worms and seeds, but also have adapted to eating the scraps they find in towns and cities.

Bald Eagle | *North America*

Bald eagles are very large brown birds with white heads, yellow hooked bills and strong talons. They feed on fish and dead animals. Pairs will often mate for life. Together, they build huge stick nests in trees or on utility poles and towers, preferably near water. Eagles were once in danger of disappearing, since the pesticide DDT caused their eggshells to thin and break. Their numbers have rebounded since the pesticide was banned.

Eastern and Western Wood-Pewee | *North America, Central America, South America*

The two wood-pewee species, eastern and western, are almost identical except for their calls. The eastern's song is a clear *pee-a-wee* sound, while the western has a sharper call. Both species have gray bodies, dark gray heads and wings, and white bellies. These birds live in or near wooded areas in North America and winter in Central or South America. Their numbers may decline with the loss of forests.

Glossary

adaptation: an evolutionary change that enables a living thing to become suited to a certain environment or way of life

aloft: in the air

banking: tilting sideways and making a turn

burrow: an underground hole or tunnel dug by an animal, often used for shelter

colony: a group of animals that live together in one place

courting: behaving in ways in order to attract a mate

dread: the sudden rising up of a group of terns

flycatcher: a bird that catches its food while flying

harass: to continually bother or annoy

hover: to remain in one place in the air

kettle: a group of hawks circling in a warm upward air current

lift: the upward force that allows a bird to fly

loitering: waiting or hanging around an area

migrate: to travel from one region or climate to another, sometimes over a long distance

mob: to attack or harass an intruding animal, often to protect offspring

murmuration: a huge flock of starlings flying together before roosting

pesticide: a substance used to destroy things seen as pests, such as certain insects

predator: an animal that preys on, or hunts and kills, other animals

prey: an animal hunted as food by another animal

roost: to settle down for rest and sleep

semipalmated: having partly webbed toes

skein: a flock of flying geese, usually in a V shape

stoop: a steep, fast dive

streamlined: having a smooth shape that can move easily through the air or water

talon: a claw on a bird of prey, such as a hawk or eagle

thermal: a rising column of warm air

thrust: a strong push in a certain direction

updraft: an upward-moving air current

venturesome: willing to take a risk or seek adventure

wheeling: flying overhead in large circles

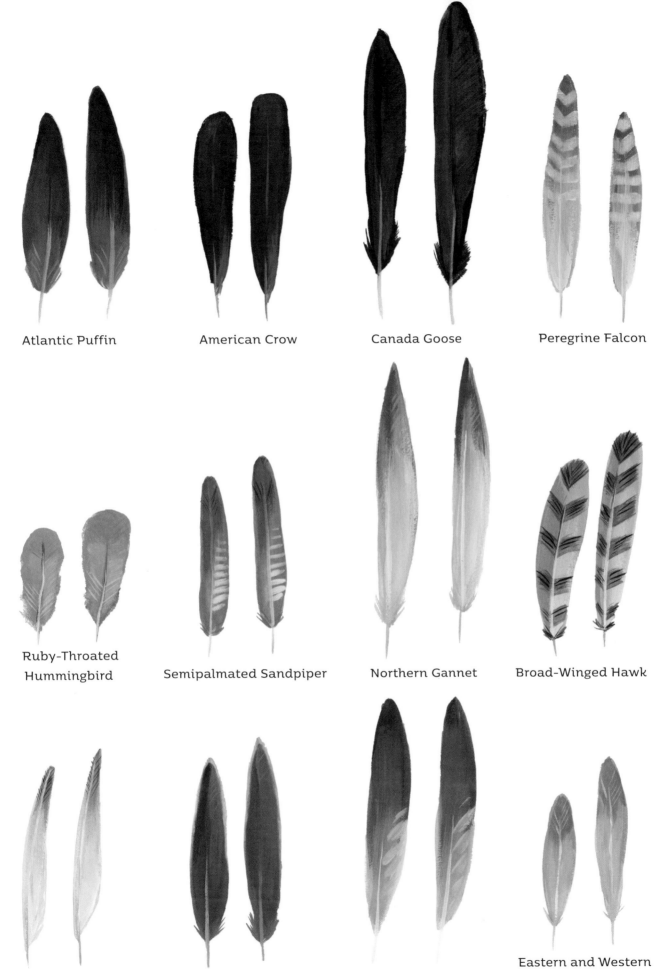

Atlantic Puffin

American Crow

Canada Goose

Peregrine Falcon

Ruby-Throated
Hummingbird

Semipalmated Sandpiper

Northern Gannet

Broad-Winged Hawk

Arctic Tern

European Starling

Bald Eagle

Eastern and Western
Wood-Pewee

For my four, who have flown — S.V.G.

For Marian and Bill — M.H.

Acknowledgments

Many thanks to Bob Montgomerie of the Biology Department at Queen's University and Ted Cheskey of Nature Canada for their review of the manuscript.

Text © 2019 Susan Vande Griek
Illustrations © 2019 Mark Hoffmann

All rights reserved. No part of this publication may be reproduced, stored in a retrieval system or transmitted, in any form or by any means, without the prior written permission of Kids Can Press Ltd. or, in case of photocopying or other reprographic copying, a license from The Canadian Copyright Licensing Agency (Access Copyright). For an Access Copyright license, visit www.accesscopyright.ca or call toll free to 1-800-893-5777.

Kids Can Press gratefully acknowledges the financial support of the Government of Ontario, through Ontario Creates; the Ontario Arts Council; the Canada Council for the Arts; and the Government of Canada for our publishing activity.

Published in Canada and the U.S. by Kids Can Press Ltd.
25 Dockside Drive, Toronto, ON M5A 0B5

Kids Can Press is a Corus Entertainment Inc. company

www.kidscanpress.com

The artwork in this book was rendered in gouache and digital media.
The text is set in Moreno.

Edited by Katie Scott
Designed by Marie Bartholomew

Printed and bound in Shenzhen, China, in 3/2019 by Imago

CM 19 0 9 8 7 6 5 4 3 2 1

Library and Archives Canada Cataloguing in Publication

Vande Griek, Susan, 1950–, author
       Hawks kettle, puffins wheel, and other poems of birds in flight
/ Susan Vande Griek & Mark Hoffmann.

ISBN 978-1-77138-995-2 (hardcover)

       1. Birds — Flight — Juvenile literature. 1. Hoffmann, Mark, 1977–, illustrator 11. Title.

QL698.7.V36 2019   j598.15'7   C2018-906089-1